Dear Parent,

The Anne of Green Gables Series was created with the aid of teachers to raise social and educational issues that will benefit young children.

Anne is a strong female character with a colorful vocabulary and a vibrant imagination. Her vocabulary level is meant to stimulate the reading experience for young people. Inserted on the final pages of this book is a handy dictionary for clarification of certain words and expressions.

Step into Anne's world and benefit from her desire to build friendships and inspire others through her wonderful imagination and her determination to succeed!

Log on to **www.learnwithanne.com** and explore an educational guide, with outlines of lesson plans and discussion topics available for teachers and parents alike.

Also check out **www.annetoon.com** for educational games, activities and multimedia that bring Anne's character and friends to life.

Anne of Green Gables

Published in 2010 by Davenport Press
110 Davenport Rd.
Toronto, Ontario, M5R 3R3

Printed in Canada   ISBN = 978-0-9736803-8-6

anne of green gables

AS SEEN ON
PBS

Anne AND THE BULLY

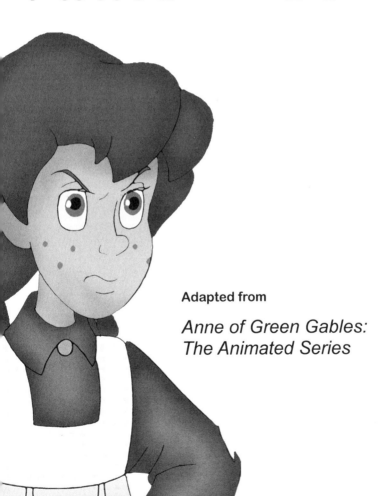

Adapted from

*Anne of Green Gables:
The Animated Series*

CONTENTS

1

Felix's Troubles

It was a long morning. Felix had been looking forward to lunchtime for hours. He was so glad it was finally here. He sat down on the front steps and opened up his lunch bag.

"Mmm, fresh bread and cheese, my favourite," he said. He opened his mouth wide. He started to take a big bite. Suddenly someone grabbed his sandwich. "Hey!" yelled Felix.

He looked up. A big guy was standing over him. It was the new student, Orville.

"Eh-heh...hi, Orville. W-what do you want?" asked Felix.

Orville grabbed Felix's lunch. Then, he gave Felix his own lunch pail. "Trades-sies today," said Orville, in a gruff voice.

"But-but that's my lunch!" said Felix. Orville

shrugged. "Have mine," he said.

Felix peered down into Orville's lunch pail. It was practically empty. He reached in and pulled out an egg. "Hard-boiled eggs? Yuck," said Felix.

Orville chewed Felix's cheese sandwich. He smiled and patted his stomach. "Mmm! I think we'll have to make this a regular habit!" he said.

Felix looked up at Orville. He wanted to protest, but Orville was so much bigger than him. What could Felix do? He sighed. He cracked the egg and took a bite. It was bland and mushy. He chewed it slowly, and forced himself to swallow. He tried to distract himself from the taste by flipping through a book about flying machines. Orville was still watching him. Felix felt like he had to say something. Finally, he looked up at Orville. "I think I'd rather not," he said.

Orville frowned at Felix. He grabbed the book, and started to look through it.

"Hey, give it back! That's mine," said Felix.

"You like these stupid flying machines?" asked Orville.

"So what if I do?" asked Felix.

"You're an egghead, you know that?" said Orville.

Felix was holding an egg. He looked down at it and frowned.

Orville pointed and snickered. "Hey look! Felix is an egghead!" he yelled. A bunch of kids looked at Felix and laughed.

The laughter drifted over to where Anne was eating with her best friend, Diana. They looked up. When Anne saw people laughing at her friend, she marched right over to their table. When she realized that Orville had been bullying Felix, she was not amused. She looked back and forth between Orville and Felix. "What's he done to you? Leave him alone," she shouted.

Orville turned to Anne. They stared at each other, eyeball to eyeball.

"You gonna make me?" asked Orville.

"It's all right, Anne. I don't care," interrupted Felix.

Anne grabbed the book from Orville.

He smiled. "See? We were only joking around," said Orville.

"It's not a joke when the other person isn't laughing," said Anne.

She handed Felix his book. Then, she led him away. "Don't pay any attention to him," she said.

"I won't," said Felix. But how could he not pay attention? Felix was very worried.

2

· ·

A Stolen Glider

Early the next morning, Felix went to Dawson's Field. He wanted to give his new flying machine a test run. He stretched his arm back, and thrust forward. The glider flew from his fingertips. It glided smooth and low, through the air, and then landed in some tall grass. "Yahoo!" yelled Felix. He ran toward the landing zone. He picked up his glider. "I've done it! The perfect landing," he said to himself.

He whisked the glider up, and ran back to where he started. "Now if I could only design one that could go high and land, then I'd have a perfect flying machine," he said.

"Boo!" Suddenly Orville popped out from behind Felix. He had been hiding in the grass.

"Whoa!" said Felix. He stopped in his tracks. Orville laughed. "Why good morning, Felix," he said, in a sickeningly sweet voice. "Did I startle you?"

Orville glanced at the model plane. Felix tried to hide it. He put it behind his back.

"Yes, I um, I was just um, testing this before school," said Felix.

"So I saw. You make that?" asked Orville.

"Yeah, out of balsa wood," said Felix. He was so proud of his model. He couldn't help but show it to Orville. "I followed the designs of these men in France and Germany who are trying to make a machine that can fly," said Felix.

Orville looked closely at the glider. He grabbed the glider from Felix. "It sounds stupid," he said.

Felix gasped. His eyes widened. Lunch was one thing. His glider was really important to him. "Orville, please. Please be careful. It's fragile."

"I just want to play with it for a while," said Orville.

"It's time for school. Please. I need it," Felix pleaded.

Orville turned to Felix. He gave him a menacing glance. "I think I'll hold onto this for a while."

"But it's mine!" said Felix.

"So? And if you tell on me..." warned Orville.

"What?" asked Felix.

"You won't see the glider again," said Orville. Felix lunged for his glider, but Orville held it out of reach. "See you later," he smirked. Then, he turned and walked away, tossing the glider in the air, and catching it again.

Felix gulped.

3

Partners

At school that day, Orville stood with a group of kids. He showed off Felix's glider. He arched his arm back and launched the glider. "See? It's a model of balsa wood, like the real gliders they make in France and Germany."

Felix sat sulking in a swing. He watched the crowd. "That's my glider he's showing off," he sighed.

Anne was swinging on the swing next to Felix. She looked at Orville. "If it's yours, why does he have it?" asked Anne.

"Uh, I lent it to him," lied Felix.

"You lent it to Orville?" asked Anne.

"The truth is, he took it from me," said Felix.

This was too much for Anne. She dug her feet into the ground, stopping her swing instantly. "That cruel oaf brazenly stole your prized model?" asked Anne.

"He said he'd give it back," said Felix.

Anne jumped up from her swing. She rolled up her sleeves. Then she marched towards Orville and the crowd. "Oh he'll give it back all right," said Anne.

Felix stood up. He grabbed Anne's sleeve, yanking her to a stop. "Wait! Anne, you can't do anything," he pleaded.

"Why not? He took your glider," said Anne.

"If he finds out I told you, well, he said I'll never see it again," said Felix.

Anne sunk back down into her swing. She shook her head.

Felix sat down beside her. "He's been picking on me since he moved here. What do I do?"

Anne rested her chin on her hand. "Just wait," she said. "He'll lose interest. And in the meantime, you can just avoid him."

Felix glanced towards Orville and the other kids. "Just don't tell him you know," he said.

Anne glanced towards Orville. He was still showing off Felix's glider to a crowd of students. She shook her head. "Felix, it will take all of my will power," she said.

The school bell blared. Anne and Felix got up from the swings. They headed towards the classroom with the rest of the kids.

...

Miss Hetty King, the school teacher, stood in front of the class and watched everyone file in. She waited for them to settle down. She looked at the clock. She was impatient because she had important news. "We're going to have a science fair," she said. "And since Avonlea hosts this year's regional fair, I expect a roster of experiments to do this town proud!'

Felix nodded. "Flying machines!" he whispered to himself.

"Now choose your partners," said Hetty.

The classroom immediately grew louder. Students shifted seats and talked to their friends, trying to find matches. Anne and Diana paired up. So did Gilbert and Perry. Felicity chose Amy to be her partner.

Hetty wandered around the classroom. "Very good, very good," she said when she noticed how quickly everyone was pairing off.

Felix was partnerless. He looked around. "What about me?" he asked. Someone tapped Felix's shoulder.

He turned around.

"How about you be my partner?" asked Orville. He was standing with Felix's glider in his hand.

"M-m-m-me?" asked Felix.

"We'll do a project on these flying machines of yours," said Orville.

Hetty smiled at Gilbert and Perry. "Volcanoes - a very good subject," she told them.

"Ours will be on the gramophone and sound recording," chirped Amy.

"Wonderful!" said Hetty. She walked over to Diana

and Anne.

Anne stood up and cleared her throat. "After much consideration in these brief seconds, Diana and I decided our project shall be on horses," said Anne.

"Hmmm, good, although you'll want to be more specific - it is a science fair, after all," said Hetty.

"But how can we be specific when the world of horses is so vast, so fascinating, so worthy of a fuller scope of discussion?" asked Anne.

Hetty glared at Anne.

Diana popped her hand on Anne's mouth. "We will certainly narrow down our topic, Miss King," she said.

Meanwhile, Orville was hovering over a very nervous Felix.

"You sure you wouldn't rather work with somebody else?" asked Felix.

Hetty walked over to the two of them. "Felix! It's so nice to see you welcoming the new boy by being his partner."

"Well, actually-" began Felix.
"And what is your subject?" interrupted Hetty.

Orville smiled at Felix. Felix sighed. "Flying

machines," he said.

"Marvelous," said Hetty. "An auspicious start!"

Anne glanced toward Felix. She saw Orville, and she knew, right away...something wasn't right.

4

Anne's Help

Orville played with Felix's glider on his way home from school. Anne had had just about enough. She ran to catch up with him.

"That's Felix's model, isn't it?" she asked.

"So what if it is? He lent it to me," said Orville.

Anne put her hands on her hips. "That's not what Felix told me," she said.

Orville stopped in his tracks. He spun around. "That pipsqueak told you?" he asked.

Anne looked up at Orville. Suddenly she had some second thoughts. But it was too late for that. She gulped.

"So what if he did? Felix is my friend. He can tell me what he likes," she said.

"Oh yeah? We'll see about that," said Orville. He

turned and walked away.

Anne watched him go. "Oh Anne, why didn't you keep your big mouth shut?" she asked herself.

...

Felix needed to cheer himself up. Later that afternoon, he treated himself to an ice cone. He strolled out of Lawson's Store. Just carrying the cherry and blueberry ice cone made everything seem better. He smiled down at it. It glistened in the sun. It looked so sweet and cold. He closed his eyes and raised it to his lips.

Whiz! A ball streaked past, knocking the ice right off of the cone.

Felix took a lick. All he tasted was a lot of air. What's going on? He looked down. The red and blue ice was splattered all over the pavement. He looked around and noticed Orville walking toward him.

"Hey squeaky, get out of my way when I'm practicing my pitching!" Orville shouted, laughing. He picked up his baseball.

This was too much for Felix to ignore. "I've been saving all week for that ice cone!" he yelled.

Orville walked closer to Felix, and stared him down.

"Oh yeah? Well it serves you right for telling on me to that redhead," he said.

"Oh no. What did Anne say now?" groaned Felix.

"Just for being a snitch, you'll have to do the science fair project all on your own," said Orville.

"But I need my glider!" shouted Felix.

"You should have thought about that before you started snitching!" said Orville. He turned and stormed off.

Felix watched him walk away. He crumpled the paper cone and threw it down. Then, he plopped down on the steps.

5

· ·

Horsing Around

Back at Green Gables, Diana and Anne worked on their science project. They took it very seriously.

"Look out for the water!" yelled Diana.

"And next comes the timber rails!" said Anne.

"Don't knock them down," said Diana.

Anne and Diana galloped through the kitchen. They both wore riding hats. They held their hands up as if they were holding reins. They jumped over a mop perched between two chairs. Then, they trotted around the kitchen through the racecourse they had created. Besides the jump, their course consisted of a bucket of water, a large sofa and a couple of leafy houseplants.

"On to the stone wall!" yelled Anne.

Anne rounded a corner, and ran by the sofa. She knocked into it, and ended up tipping the sofa on its side.

"Oh! My poor horse knocked over a whole stone wall!" she said.

The girls giggled. Then, they 'galloped' around the kitchen table and jumped over a houseplant perched on a chair.

"You can make up points with the hedge!" said Diana.

Suddenly Matthew, Anne's adoptive father, stepped into the kitchen. "Ah hem," he coughed.

The girls looked up, surprised. They started to laugh.

"Huh?" asked Matthew, looking around at the mess.

The girls fell into each other, knocking over a chair in the process. The plant, which rested on it, catapulted right towards Matthew. Lucky for them, he caught it.

"Oh, Matthew. Forgive us. We were practicing steeplechase, and we... we..." Anne was out of breath. She didn't know what to say.

"We got a bit out of control," finished Diana.

Matthew put the plant down in the center of the table. "A steeplechase, eh? The sport of queens."

"Exactly. We're doing research for our science fair," said Anne.

Matthew righted the sofa. "You'd best not be caught 'researching' in here. He told the girls that his sister Marilla, Anne's adoptive mother, would be back from Mrs. Lynde's any minute.

"Uh-oh," said Anne.

"Oh dear," said Diana.

The girls scrambled to put the chairs back in the living room.

"You see, Matthew, we're trying to narrow down our idea," said Anne.

"Horses are a very big subject," said Diana.

"It's good to, er, exercise your options. But keep it to the kitchen," said Matthew.

Crash! What was that? The three of them went to see about the noise. It was coming from the kitchen. They stopped at the doorway. Marilla was home. She stepped straight into the bucket of water.

6

Changing Tactics

Anne went to Felix's house first thing the next morning. She knocked on the front door. It opened just a crack. Felix peeked out.

"Oh, good morning, Anne," he said.

"I'll walk to school with you so you can avoid any mishaps. And speaking of mishaps, you'll never guess what fiasco I caused last night…" said Anne.

Felix frowned. He opened the door completely. He was still wearing his pajamas.

"Felix! You're not even dressed for school," said Anne.

"I'm not going to school today," said Felix.

"Why ever not?" asked Anne.

"I'm not feeling well," said Felix.

"Oh come now..." said Anne.

"I'm not! I...I have a cough," said Felix. He put his hand to his throat. He forced a small cough. "See?" he insisted.

"Felix, I know you're fibbing," said Anne. "All right. The truth is, I never want to go to school again so long as Orville is there," confessed Felix.

"Faking a cough for the next ten years is hardly a practical strategy," said Anne.

Felix flopped down into a chair on the porch. He

threw up his hands. "You said I should avoid him," he said.

Anne sat down next to Felix. "I admit, our first tactic wasn't the best," she said.

"And then you went and told him," said Felix.

Anne cringed. She felt guilty. But she had just been trying to help. "I couldn't help it, it just leapt from my lips! That's why I'm determined to help you, Felix," she said. "Look on the bright side. At least you have a science fair project. All Diana and I have is a vague horsy idea and Marilla's wet shoes to contend with!"

Felix looked up at Anne. "Wet shoes?" he asked.

"I'll explain on the way. What do you say? You've got friends to stand by you," she told him.

Felix smiled. "Okay. Just let me get changed," he said.

1

Felix's Dilemma

Diana, Anne and Felix raced to school. They galloped as if they were horses in a race.

"Uh-oh! And Flying Leap takes the lead!" shouted Anne.

"Ha, ha, look at him go. He's headed for the finish line. It's Flying Leap and Ginger Snap," yelled Felix. He was already feeling better. "Flying Leap…"

Suddenly, Diana took the lead. "And Raven Locks! Up the inside, she takes the lead for the finish!" she yelled.

The three of them sprinted past a tree. Diana managed to finish first. After crossing the finish line, they flopped themselves down on the side of the road. They huffed and puffed to catch their breath.

"Good run, Raven Locks!" said Anne.

"Whew! Anne I'm not sure about horse racing as a science fair subject," said Diana.

"I suppose not," said Anne. "We might encourage the unspeakable vice of gambling. Oh Diana, what are we going to do?"

"We'll think of something," said Diana.

Felix looked at his friends. "You two will have fun no matter what the topic. I have to do my whole project myself," said Felix.

Anne sat up. Now she was mad. "That's the absolute apex of unfairness! And all because of Orville."

"I don't mind, really," said Felix.

Anne stood up. She brushed the grass off of her knees. Then, she helped her friends up. "That does it. We're telling Miss King," she said.

Felix grabbed Anne's arm. "No! You can't!" he said.

"Felix, Orville is taking advantage of you," said Diana.

"If we tell the teacher, Orville will only take it out on me. Look what happened when Anne talked to him," said Felix.

"You're right," said Anne. She shook her head. "What a complex and frightful dilemma!"

8

A New Bully

At school that morning, Orville was on the see-saw with Perry. "I worked so hard on our project. If I'd known what a slouch Felix is, I never would have teamed up with him," said Orville.

"That's a lie and you know it," said Anne's voice. Orville turned. Anne was glaring at him, her hands on her hips.

Orville laughed, nervously, from the top of the see-saw. "What are you talking about?" he asked.

He tried to see-saw down, but Anne wouldn't let him. She put all her weight on the bar. Orville was stuck. And now, a crowd had gathered. A group of students watched the scene.

"Go ahead!" Anne shouted to him. "Try and come up with one single solitary thing that you've done on this science project."

"Well, I, uh," Orville stuttered. "It's very complex."

"Complex, my foot! Orville, you ought to be ashamed of yourself," said Anne.

Orville looked at the crowd of kids. They were all staring at him. He started to panic. "I've done plenty. Now let me go!" he yelled.

Anne took her weight off of the see-saw.

Orville came crashing down. He looked past Anne to Felix, who was cowering in the background. "You're going to be sorry, Felix!" he yelled. Then, he stormed into school.

Felix gasped in fright.

...

After spending the entire day avoiding Orville, Felix needed to escape. As soon as the school bell rang, he ran off to Dawson's Field. He had made a new model glider and he wanted to give it a test fly. He found the perfect spot to launch it. It flew beautifully through the air, low along the grass.

"The lunchtime launch is a success! The new design gets great distance!" said Felix.

The landing was a different story. The glider tumbled to the ground, and flipped over. Felix ran to pick it up. "If only I could get both distance and a good landing in one design," he said.

He inspected his plane for damage. It seemed to be in good shape. Felix heard some footsteps behind him. He spun around. It was Orville.

"Uh-oh," groaned Felix, under his breath.

"What's this, a new model?" asked Orville.

"I-I-I'm sorry Anne said that," said Felix.

Orville wasn't paying attention to Felix. He was too excited about the new glider. "Nice work," he said. "I'll have to test it." Orville grabbed the glider and started to walk away with it.

"Hey!" said Felix.

Luckily Anne and Diana were just approaching them. "Give him back his glider right now!" shouted Anne.

"What? I'm only looking," said Orville.

Anne pushed Orville. "You're a bully. You know that?" she said.

"I am not!" shouted Orville.

Anne pushed Orville again. This time, she

knocked him to the ground.

"Ooof!" he said, when he landed.

"Don't you dare deny it!" she said. She stood over Orville and yelled. "You made Felix do all of the work. You stole his glider. You scared him so bad he didn't want to go to school. That's the work of a stinking rat!" said Anne.

Orville looked at Anne. Her face was red. She was furious. His eyes opened wide, in terror. He was so scared and surprised. He didn't know what to say.

Anne tried to pry the glider from his hands. A creak came from the wing.

"No!" said Felix.

It creaked again, as Anne struggled to grab the glider from Orville's hands.

"Anne," said Diana.

"You give it back!" Anne shouted.

"Wait, be careful, it's," - began Orville.

Crack! The glider snapped in half.

"Fragile," finished Orville.

Anne looked at the wrecked plane in her hand. What had she done? Her eyes welled up with tears. She looked at Felix, Orville and Diana. "Now look what you made me do!" she shouted. She dropped the broken glider and ran off.

Anne ran all the way to Barry's Pond. She sat on the bridge with tears in her eyes. Her legs dangled over. She stared at the water and thought about the mess.

Diana found her soon after.

Anne looked up at her friend. "That Orville is the worst bully imaginable."

"He is. But Anne, you were mean to him too," said Diana.

"Only because he was mean to Felix," said Anne.

"You won't help Felix by behaving like Orville yourself," said Diana.

"Me, behave like Orville? I would never!" gasped Anne.

"Anne, you were. You were being a bully. Just like him," said Diana.

9

························

Matthew's Story

Anne walked home slowly. She could hardly believe the mess they were in. Was it really all her fault? Had she behaved as badly as Orville? Didn't he deserve it?

"Anne, hey Anne!" called Felix. He ran up to her. "You sure showed Orville," he said.

"I also broke your glider," said Anne.

"Aw, you didn't mean to," said Felix.

"And even worse, I was mean to him. As mean as he was to you!" said Anne.

"So? He deserved it," Felix insisted.

"Felix, nobody deserves to be picked on," said Anne. She shook her head. "I've only made matters worse. He'll still pick on you, worse than ever," she said.

Felix looked at Anne. "Oh no. So, what do we do

now?" he asked.

"I wish I knew," said Anne.

When Anne, Diana and Felix came to a crossroad, they parted ways. Anne walked to Green Gables. She noticed Matthew, in the distance. He was plowing in the fields, with the Sorrel Mare. She brought him a bucket of water.

"Whoa! There's a good girl," Matthew was saying to the horse. He looked up and noticed Anne.

"Why, it's the water maiden!" he said.

Anne giggled. She handed Matthew the bucket. He took a sip from the ladle. Then he placed the bucket in front of the mare so that she could drink.

"There you go, girl. She's thirsty today," he said.

Anne watched Matthew pet the horse.

"The Sorrel Mare is so much bigger and stronger than you. Are you ever afraid she'll be mean to you?" asked Anne.

"I treat a horse with respect. I make sure I never get frustrated or impatient or cruel. That's the only way we can work together," said Matthew.

"But I wonder," Anne said. She bit her lip. "What if a person's so mean you can't work with him?"

"You mean what if the person's a bully?" asked Matthew.

"Exactly," said Anne.

Matthew nodded. He pointed to an old, run-down doghouse, which sat at the edge of the field. "See that old doghouse over there?" he said.

"Yes?" said Anne.

"That was here when Marilla and I moved to Green Gables. It was years ago, when we were kids. A dog

lived there then."

"Old Rex was a mean old mutt when we found him here," said Matthew. "He was afraid of people. He growled and snarled whenever anyone tried to come near. It took a long time, but after a while I got to trust him. Of course, it wasn't so easy for everyone. But eventually, I was able to walk the dog, and to run with him through the fields. With a lot of patience and kindness, Old Rex came to see we didn't mean him any harm. He lived out his days a nice old dog - man's best friend - or at least this little boy's."

"Astounding," said Anne.

"You think so?" asked Matthew.

"Yes! I can't imagine you or Marilla ever being young," said Anne.

Matthew laughed. "It happens to us all, as far as I know."

"So why do you suppose the dog was mean in the first place?" asked Anne.

Matthew scratched his head. "Well, I figure the previous owners were mean to him. They did abandon him here after all. They never played with him, so he got sadder and sadder and more and more ornery, until he was grumpy all the time," said Matthew.

Anne found an old rusty chair in the dust. She picked it up and studied it. "So really, he just needed someone to be nice to him," she said.

"A little kindness goes a long way," said Matthew.

Anne noticed Diana walking towards her. "Thanks Matthew. You have helped immeasurably," said Anne.

Matthew shrugged. He turned back to his plowing.

Anne ran over to Diana.
"I wondered if you were up to working on our project,"

said Diana.

"I've never been more inspired!" said Anne.

Diana looked at Anne. "What happened?" she asked. "Last time I saw you, you were all glum."

"Diana, not only have I realized how to help Felix with Orville tomorrow, but I have the most thrilling idea on what to do about the science project!" said Anne.

10

· ·

Being Mean

Felix went to Dawson's Field early the next morning. He threw up a new glider. This one did a loop-de-loop, then nose-dived into the grass. He sighed, and threw his hands up in the air. He was so disappointed.

"Well, this model can't fly or land," he said.

Orville sneaked up behind Felix. "What a dud!" he said.

Felix ignored him. He tried another throw. The plane started out okay. It looped again, and then it came crashing down.

"What's the matter? Are you deaf?" asked Orville.

Felix picked up the glider. He adjusted the flaps. "No. I'm just going to ignore you if you speak to me that way," he said.

"I'm only joking around," said Orville.

"Well I don't find it funny," said Felix.

Orville watched Felix work with the plane. "What are you doing?" he asked.

"Finding the right mixture of lift and stability," Felix replied.

"I don't understand," said Orville.

"That's because you haven't done a lick of work on this whole project," said Felix.

"Then tell me what you're doing so I don't look like a dummy at the science fair tomorrow," said Orville.

Felix tucked his model plane into his book bag. "I have a better idea," he said. "Why don't you do your own science project."

"What?" asked Orville.

"I don't want you as a partner," said Felix. He turned and walked away.

"But, wait!" Orville shouted. "You have to! You'll be sorry!"

Felix turned. "We'll see about that," he said. He continued to walk away.

Orville stood at Dawson's Field, alone. "Now what do I do?" he asked himself.

Later that day, Anne ran into Felix. He was storming down Main Street. His face was bright red.

"What's wrong?" asked Anne.

"I hate him! That numbskull will see how he likes it without a partner!" said Felix.

"Being mean back won't help. He'll only be meaner to you," said Anne.

"What else can I do?" asked Felix.

"It's time we took some constructive action," said Anne. She led Felix towards the Town Hall. "First off, we tell Miss King."

Felix dragged his heels. "What? No way!" he shouted.

"Felix, we need some help on this - and she's the one to give it to us," said Anne.

"Are you sure?" asked Felix.

"Yes, let's go," said Anne.

||

A New Plan

Anne and Felix walked into the Town Hall. The place was packed with townspeople. Everyone was busy preparing for the fair.

Hetty stood underneath a giant banner. She directed her two assistants, who were hanging it. "Higher, higher … perfect!" she said. She clapped her hands together and smiled. "I just know we're going to dazzle the jury and take top prizes!"

Anne and Felix walked over to her. "Anne! Felix! Don't you have experiments to experiment with? Calculations to calculate? Charts to chart?" asked Hetty.

"Alas, Miss King, the direst of necessities brings us here," said Anne.

"Why, whatever is the matter?" asked Hetty.

Anne elbowed Felix. "Tell her," she whispered.

"Miss King?" said Felix. "Orville is bullying me."

"I never would have guessed," said Hetty.

"Truth is, he's been mean to me since he moved to Avonlea. And it's only been getting worse," said Felix.

"You wouldn't believe the wily ways of this dastardly miscreant," said Anne.

Hetty nodded. "I get the picture, Anne. While I am surprised, Felix, you may rest assured I'll keep an eye on the boy and put a stop to any inappropriate behaviour," said Hetty.

"Golly, Miss King. Thank you!" said Felix.

"If necessary, I'll also remove him from your science fair project," said Hetty.

Felix gave the possibility a moment of thought. "I don't think that will be necessary," he said.

"But Felix, you said before…" started Anne.

"If you feel the least bit unsure…" said Hetty.

Felix shook his head. "Miss King, I appreciate your offer. But I'd like to see if I can make things work. I have an idea," he said.

"How noble!" said Anne.

An hour later, Felix stood in the barn at Green Gables. "I'm not going to fight you," he said. "I want you to treat me properly." Felix stood tall. He was acting very brave. Of course, he was face to face with the scarecrow. "You have no reason to be mean to me. I never hurt you." He reached out to the scarecrow. "Why can't we just be friends?" he asked.

Anne stood up and clapped. "That was flawless. Great job! You'll tame the savage beast, yet!" she congratulated.

Diana popped her head inside the barn. "Come on, Anne. It's time to put the finishing touches on our project," she said.

"Oh, Diana, you just missed the most marvelous performance," said Anne.

Felix grinned.

12

Teamwork

The Town Hall was all dressed up for the science fair that was going to be that evening. Some of the students were just starting to arrive, to drop off their projects.

Hetty noticed Orville. She frowned. "If you're going to loiter around, Orville, you may as well pass me those trophies," she said.

Orville passed Hetty three trophies. "Miss King?" he said. "I need another partner for the science fair," he said.

"Oh? What happened to Felix?" she asked.

"He's just not pulling his weight," shrugged Orville.

"Now I'm going to stop you right there before you say something you really regret," said Hetty.

Orville was taken aback.

"You know what happens to bullies?" asked Hetty. "They end up without any friends, not knowing how to get along with others, and most never know the reward of doing their own work. Of course, only you have the power to change your behaviour."

"Yes, Ma'am," said Orville. He slouched away.

Hetty noticed Felix's broken glider in his book bag. "Hmmm," she said.

...

Back at Green Gables, Anne and Diana were putting the finishing touches on their display. Their project was about the history of raising horses - horse husbandry. There was even a tiny model of Matthew and the Sorrel Mare.

"Wonderful diagrams, Diana," said Anne.

"A superior model, Anne," said Diana.

"Horse and human," began Anne.

"What a team!" finished Diana.

...

Back at the King house, Felix sat on his porch working on his display. Orville walked up to him.

Felix looked up, noticed Orville and said nothing. Orville pulled the broken glider from his bag. He put it beside the two that Felix was working on.

"What's this?" asked Felix.

"I fixed the broken glider," said Orville. He picked it up to show Felix. "Only, I made an adjustment here."

"Yeah?" said Felix.

"Yeah, it flies well," said Orville. He threw it into the air. The model glided along smoothly.

Felix shook his head. "That one was designed to fly well. But it doesn't land worth stink," he said.

"It does now," said Orville.

Suddenly the model touched down into a perfect landing.

Felix's jaw dropped. He ran over to the plane. "How did you do that?" he asked.

"I bent the wings," said Orville. "It keeps it stable."

"This is great!" said Felix.

Orville smiled. He was proud of his work. "I admit I've been interested in flying machines myself. I just had no idea of how to start one."

"Well, you're a natural," said Felix.

"Thanks!" said Orville.

Orville and Felix looked at each other. They were so used to being enemies. They didn't know how they were supposed to act.

"Does this mean we're a team?" asked Orville.

"Just as long as you don't bully me," said Felix.

"I won't. I promise," said Orville.

"Then we'd better get to work," said Felix.

They smiled and then began to work on their display.

13

. . . .

The Science Fair

The Town Hall was packed with science experiments. Pans bubbled over. Kinetic demonstrations zipped by. Electricity sparked. Lava bubbled.

Felicity and Amy made their own wax recording. When they cranked the record handle, it produced their poem… "Sounds of the rude world heard in the day, lulled by moonlight have all passed away."

Anne and Diana's display about horses and humans looked great.

Felix and Orville explained their project. A group of judges watched. The three gliders formed the centre-piece of their display.

"And as you can see, we kept the best of the 'distance' design," said Felix.

"With the best of a 'smooth landing' design," said Orville.

"To get," said Felix.

"A perfect flying machine," both boys finished together.

Hetty joined the judges. "Nice work, boys," she said.

They both smiled. Anne winked at Felix and picked

up Orville's model.

"Who would have guessed that your accident would be such a good thing," said Orville.

"Life is full of surprises, Orville. I guess people are, too," said Anne.

They smiled. Suddenly, they heard a bang. Everyone looked at Gilbert and Perry's project. They had made a papier-mâché volcano. It exploded loudly, sputtering lava in all directions.

Everyone laughed.

14

. . . .

New Friends

Felix and Orville sat on the front steps of the Town Hall. They admired their small trophy.

"With some last-minute teamwork, we pulled it off," said Felix.

"Next year, we'll get first prize," said Orville.

"You think so?" asked Felix.

"We've got all year for test flights," said Orville.

Felix handed Orville the trophy. "You want to take this home first?" he asked.

"No. You deserve it. You did most of the work," said Orville.

"Who knows, maybe one day we will invent a way to fly people in gliders like this," said Felix. He

gazed up at the sky.

"Wouldn't that be a strange sight!" said Orville. He pulled some cookies out of his book bag.

Felix eyed them. He handed Orville the trophy.

"Trade-sies?" he asked.

Orville shrugged. He accepted the trophy and handed Felix a cookie.

They both munched on cookies. Felix threw the glider into the air. And together, they watched it soar.

Anne's Fancy Dancy Words

● ●

Amused – to find something funny
Apex – a limit or point
Astounding – very surprising
Auspicious – when something or someone looks like
                   they will turn out well
Balsa – a light wood used for toy airplanes
Bland – boring
Blared – when a sound rings very loudly
Brazenly – to act like you do not care
Catapulted – fly towards
Complex – difficult or hard to understand
Constructive – helpful, worth doing
Cringed – a facial expression showing displeasure
Dastardly – cowardly, sneaky
Deaf – unable to hear
Dilemma – a problem or conflict
Direst – very important, urgent
Dud – something that doesn't work
Fiasco – disaster, problem
Galloped – to move like a horse
Glared – to stare at someone
Glum – sad, depressed
Lunged – a sudden movement forward or
                towards something
Kinetic – motion or movement

Loiter – to hang around a place for no particular reason
Maiden – young woman
Menacing – scary
Miscreant – a villain
Mutt - dog
Mishap – a mistake, when something doesn't go right
Narrow – to make something smaller
Necessities – things that need to exist or happen
Numbskull – someone who is not very smart
Oaf – someone who is not very smart
Ornery – someone or something that is not nice to be around
Pleaded – to beg, try to convince
Roster – a list
Savage – like an animal
Scope – a range or boundary
Snitch – someone who tells on another person
Solitary – single, only one
Sprinted – ran fast
Sputtering – spitting, ejecting
Startle – to scare or frighten someone unexpectedly
Strategy – a plan
Streaked – to fly by
Tactic – a plan of action
Thrust – to push or shove
Vague – not specific, very general
Vast – large, huge, enormous
Vice – a bad habit
Whisked – to carry or move something quickly
Wily – sneaky, tricky